Disney

Anna & Elsa

The Secret Admirer

For G.L.O.W.,
and Gorgeous Ladies of Writing
the world over!
—E.D.

randomhousekids.com

ISBN 978-0-7364-3475-1 (hc) — ISBN 978-0-7364-8210-3 (lib. bdg.)

Printed in the United States of America

10 9 8 7 6 5 4 3 2 1

DISNEY

Anna & Elsa

The Secret Admirer

By Erica David
Illustrated by Bill Robinson,
Manuela Razzi, Francesco Legramandi,
and Gabriella Matta

Random House New York

Chapter 1

"I found it!" Olaf shouted. The cheerful snowman stood in the middle of a field of tall grass. The grass was waving in the warm spring breeze. Olaf waved, too— with one hand, he waved to Anna and Elsa. With the other, he waved a long, pointy carrot.

"Thank goodness!" said Elsa. She and

Anna had been helping Olaf search for his carrot nose. The nose had gone missing during a game of hide-and-seek. Elsa was relieved that the search was over. They'd been looking for almost an hour. She and Anna watched as Olaf smooshed his nose back onto his face.

"I guess I love hide-and-seek so much, my nose wanted to hide, too!" Olaf exclaimed.

"Your nose is better at hiding than you are. It only took me five minutes to find you!" Anna joked. She tweaked the carrot playfully back into place.

"Mystery solved!" Olaf declared.

"Just in time for dinner. Is anyone else hungry?" Anna asked.

Elsa's stomach rumbled in response. "That's a yes," she replied. She linked arms with her sister, grabbed Olaf's hand, and led them back toward the castle.

As soon as they walked through the castle gates, Kai, Anna and Elsa's loyal longtime servant, greeted them.

"Good afternoon, Your Majesty," Kai said. "A special delivery came for you."

"Delivery? But I'm not expecting anything," Elsa said. "Who's it from?"

"I've no idea," Kai replied. He led Elsa, Anna, and Olaf to Elsa's study. There, sitting on her desk, was a lumpy box wrapped in wrinkled brown paper. The package was clumsily tied with a piece of ribbon.

"Must be a surprise," Anna said, looking at the strange parcel.

"A mystery!" Olaf squealed. He clapped his tree-branch hands together.

Elsa was curious. She lifted the package in both hands and shook it. Something solid thudded against the inside. Anna leaned forward for a closer look. Suddenly, she wrinkled her nose.

"What's that smell?" she asked.

Elsa brought the package closer to her face and sniffed. "Hmmm, it's kind of . . . salty. It reminds me a little of . . . the sea," she said thoughtfully.

"The sea?" Olaf asked. His eyes widened. "I know who sent it! Pirates!"

"Why would pirates send Elsa a package?" asked Anna.

Olaf shrugged. "Pirates are very mysterious."

Kai scratched his chin, considering. "There is one way to find out," he said.

"What's that?" Olaf asked.

Kai and Elsa exchanged a glance and she nodded. "I could just open the package," she said.

"Great idea!" Olaf agreed. He and Anna drew closer in anticipation. Elsa carefully untied the ribbon, then gently peeled the wrinkled brown paper from the box. She lifted the lid of the box—and found an oblong object wrapped in more paper. She

picked up the object and was surprised to find that it was cold. Very cold.

"What could it be?" Anna asked eagerly.

Elsa shrugged. She was still baffled. Cautiously, she removed the paper. In her hands was a frozen fish!

"Oh!" Elsa said, surprised. "I didn't expect that. Maybe it's for the chef?"

"I don't think so," Kai said. "There was a note attached." He pointed out a small card in a handmade envelope attached to the paper. Elsa's name was written on it in shaky letters. Intrigued, Elsa opened the card. Inside, it said:

I'd swim against the current for you.

"Who's it from?" Anna asked, bubbling over with enthusiasm.

"It's signed 'Your Secret Admirer,'" Elsa replied.

"A secret admirer? I love secret admirers!" Olaf exclaimed. "What's a secret admirer?" he whispered to Anna.

Anna chuckled. "A secret admirer is

8

someone who likes you, but you don't know who it is."

"So it's still a mystery?" Olaf said.

"Exactly," Anna answered. "A very interesting mystery."

Anna tried to think about who would send Elsa a gift. There were plenty of people who liked the queen—the whole village, in fact! But no one stood out in particular.

"Any ideas who it could be?" she asked Elsa.

"I don't know," Elsa said, puzzled. It was nice to be liked, but also a little embarrassing.

Anna furrowed her brow. She was deep in thought. "Who would give you a frozen fish? It seems like an odd gift for an official suitor."

"An official suitor! I love official suitors!" said Olaf. "What's an official suitor?" he whispered to Anna.

"Someone who really likes a queen or a princess," Anna replied. "Though sometimes official suitors aren't what they appear to be. You remember Hans."

Olaf liked everyone and everything, but even Olaf did not like Hans of the Southern Isles. "Yuck," he said.

"Yuck is right," Anna said, chuckling in agreement. "But most suitors are perfectly nice. In fairy tales, sometimes a princess and a suitor even fall in love."

Olaf didn't need to ask Anna to explain

that. "I *love* love!" he said exuberantly.

"Me too," Anna said, smiling. "Maybe the person who sent the fish is going to ride in on a white horse and sweep Elsa off her feet, just like in a fairy tale!"

"I think we're getting a little carried away," Elsa said. "It's just a fish."

"A *love* fish," Olaf pointed out.

"Actually, it looks like a salmon," Anna replied dryly.

"What should I do with the love fish, Your Majesty?" Kai asked lightheartedly.

Elsa's stomach rumbled again. "Let's take it to the kitchen. Maybe we can have it for dinner."

"But you can't eat the love fish!" Olaf protested.

"Yes, it's a clue!" Anna agreed. "It will help us search for the secret admirer!"

"I think we've had enough searching for one day," Elsa said softly, tapping Olaf's carrot nose. She rewrapped the fish and handed it to Kai.

Olaf slumped.

"Don't worry, Olaf," Anna whispered, patting him gently. "The thing about secret admirers is they never stay secret for long."

Chapter 2

The next day, Anna and Elsa were eating lunch when Olaf bounded into the castle dining room. "Ooh, guess what!" he said cheerfully. "There's another gift from Elsa's secret admirer!"

Kai walked slowly into the room behind Olaf. He was carrying a heavy ice sculpture.

"Oh my goodness!" Elsa said, shocked.

Kai stumbled forward and placed the sculpture in the middle of the table. It was carved in the shape of a lady's head.

"Is that you?" Anna asked Elsa, who rose from her seat to take a better look.

"I'm not sure," Elsa answered. She peered closely at the face. The features were hard to make out, especially because the ice was beginning to melt. "I think so. It looks like she has a braid."

"You're right!" Anna said.

"Was there a note?" Elsa asked.

Olaf waved a rolled-up piece of paper in his tiny twig arms. "There was!" he said. "Open it! Maybe the identity of

your secret admirer will be revealed." He handed the paper to Elsa.

Elsa unrolled it and read:

"You're so nice, I carved you in ice!"

"Who is it?" Olaf asked, barely able to hold in his excitement.

"It's the same signature," Elsa replied. *"Your Secret Admirer."*

Anna was just a curious as Olaf was. She asked Elsa for the note and studied it thoroughly. "It looks like the same handwriting as the last note."

"Maybe it's the same person!" said Olaf.

"I'd say you're right," Anna agreed. "And is it just me, or does the handwriting look like someone who hasn't been writing for very long?"

"What do you mean?" Olaf asked.

Elsa moved closer to Anna and looked at the wobbly lettering. "I think she means maybe this note came from a young person," said Elsa. She turned to the butler. "Kai, where did you find this gift?"

"The same place we found the fish, Your Majesty. By one of the fountains in

17

the castle courtyard," answered Kai.

"Did anyone see who dropped it off?" Elsa said.

"Unfortunately, no," he replied. "There was a lot of activity in the courtyard this morning. The harvesters made an ice delivery, and the fishermen delivered food to the kitchen."

"Curious," Elsa said, thinking it over.

"I'll say," Anna agreed.

"I've figured it out!" Olaf exclaimed. "It was carved with magic!"

Anna looked at the statue again. To her it looked like it had been made by hand, not magic. She could even see the chisel marks in the ice. Whoever had carved it was definitely a beginner at that, too.

The statue was a bit lopsided. It didn't exactly look like Elsa, but it was clear that someone had worked very hard on it.

Anna gently pointed out the chisel marks to Olaf. "I'm afraid there's nothing magical about this statue," she explained. "It's clearly handmade."

"And as far as I know, I'm the only one in the kingdom with magic," Elsa said.

Olaf frowned. "Maybe the secret admirer likes snow?" he suggested.

"It's possible," Anna replied. "But this is Arendelle. Everyone likes snow."

Olaf hopped to his snowball feet. He paced back and forth in thought. "Maybe the secret admirer loves ice? Like . . . like an ice harvester? Or maybe the secret

admirer is *made* of ice and snow? Aha!" Olaf cried, looking down at his frosty belly. "Maybe *I'm* the secret admirer!"

"Relax, Olaf," Elsa said, amused. "I'm pretty sure you'd know if you were my secret admirer."

"Oh, right. I guess I would," Olaf replied.

Kai picked up the sculpture. "I'll put this in the portrait hall, Your Majesty. It'll make a nice addition . . . until it melts," he said.

"Thank you, Kai," Elsa responded. He lumbered out of the room carrying the queen's latest gift. Elsa followed. She was due to meet the villagers in the audience chamber after lunch. Every week, the

people of Arendelle visited the castle to ask the queen for advice.

Once Elsa was gone, Anna turned to Olaf. "Let's find out who the secret admirer is!" she said.

"Yes!" Olaf agreed. "But how?"

Anna folded her arms across her chest, considering. Both of Elsa's gifts had been found in the castle courtyard. Maybe the secret admirer was someone who lived or worked in the castle! It was as good a place as any to start.

"Why don't we begin close to home?" Anna said.

"Home is where the start is!" Olaf said.

"Or something like that," Anna answered. She led Olaf out of the dining room and into a corridor. The castle was huge, with plenty of nooks and crannies. It was an easy place for a secret admirer to hide. Luckily, Anna knew every inch of the castle. She knew just where to begin.

Chapter 3

"Wow!" Olaf said when Anna revealed the entrance to a secret passageway in her bedroom. It was hidden behind a large wardrobe. Together Anna and Olaf had pushed the heavy wardrobe aside. On the wall behind the wardrobe was a narrow panel. At first Olaf hadn't seen it. It blended in with the delicately patterned wallpaper.

"Where's the secret door?" he'd asked eagerly.

"Right here," Anna had answered. She ran her fingers along a seam in the wall. Olaf watched her carefully. After a moment, the outline of the panel became clear.

Anna had pushed the panel open to reveal the dark passageway. She picked up a candle from a small side table and stepped inside. Olaf followed, thrilled by this discovery.

"I've known about the castle's secret passageways since I was little," Anna explained. "One day, when I was no more than four, Elsa and I were playing hide-

and-seek. I ducked behind one of the tapestries in the gallery and accidentally fell through a secret door."

"That's amazing!" Olaf said.

Anna nodded. "Elsa and I explored the passageways when we first discovered them, but it's been a long time since I've been in here," she said.

"I guess that explains the cobwebs," Olaf pointed out, swatting at a pesky one overhead.

Anna shrugged. "Secret passageways are way more fun to explore than they are to clean," she joked.

The passage widened slightly up ahead, so Anna and Olaf were able to walk side by side. "We're almost there," Anna whispered.

"Almost where?" asked Olaf.

"Our first place to investigate," Anna replied. She made a left turn along the corridor and disappeared into the darkness. Olaf hurried to keep up. When he finally spotted her, Anna was leaning into a wall, looking through an opening.

"A hole!" Olaf cried excitedly.

"Shhh!" Anna whispered. "We're right beside the kitchen."

Anna lifted Olaf so he could see through the square panel in the wall. On the other side, a baker and his assistants rushed back and forth, busily preparing something very important.

"More flour! Quickly!" the baker bellowed. Two assistants picked up a heavy tin of flour between them. They carried it to a large mixing bowl sitting in the middle of the kitchen table and dumped the flour into the bowl.

"Now the eggs!" the baker cried. Another assistant stepped forward. She cracked three eggs into the bowl while the baker stirred the mixture with a heavy wooden spoon.

"That looks delicious," Olaf murmured.

"Let me see," Anna said in a hushed voice. She set Olaf down gently and peeped through the hole.

The assistants were adding sugar to mixture.

"Easy! It must be perfect!" the baker said. "It's her favorite!" He stirred the batter diligently, whipping the spoon through it until it was smooth.

"What are they making?" Olaf asked.

"I think it's some kind of cake," Anna told him.

"Cake? Why? Is it someone's birthday?" said Olaf.

Anna knew that no one was celebrating a birthday in the castle that week. "That can't be it," she said.

"Then who's it for?" Olaf whispered urgently. "The baker said it's *her* favorite."

"Good question," Anna replied. Queen Marisol of Eldora was supposed to visit next week, but the baker wouldn't make a cake for her a week in advance. As far as Anna knew, there were no special guests dining at the castle that night, and there was no reason to make a special dessert, unless . . . "Olaf, that cake has to be for Elsa! The baker must be her secret admirer!"

"WE FOUND HIM!" Olaf shouted happily.

"Shhhh!" Anna told him.

In the kitchen, the baker stopped stirring. He cocked his head and listened carefully. "Did you hear something?" he asked his assistants. They all shook their heads. Everyone was focused on preparing the batter. After a moment, the baker returned to work. He and his assistants added more ingredients to the mixture.

Soon the baker pulled several round griddles from a nearby cupboard. He placed them over the fire to heat them. When they were nice and warm, he lifted the heavy mixing bowl. He poured the batter into cake pans. Anna thought he did it lovingly, just like a secret admirer would.

Eager to find out the truth, Anna

showed Olaf a secret panel that opened into the kitchen. She quietly pushed open the panel. She and Olaf slipped into the kitchen without the busy bakers noticing. They were absorbed in pouring the batter into the last pan.

"Aha! We've got you!" Olaf announced.

The baker and his assistants were so startled, they nearly leaped out of their skin.

"For the love of strudel!" the baker cried in shock. "Where on earth did you come from?"

"That's a secret!" Olaf responded. "But you know all about secrets, don't you?" The bubbly snowman gave the baker a knowing look.

The baker frowned in confusion. He glanced at Anna, hoping she could explain. Anna returned his questioning stare with a sly smile.

"We're on to you," she said. "We know all about your gifts."

"Gifts?" he asked blankly. "Well, it's true that I'm a very gifted baker, but I'm not sure I understand."

"You know what we're talking about," Anna replied with a wink.

"No . . . I don't," the baker said. "What is going on here?"

Olaf couldn't contain himself any longer. He clapped his hands together excitedly. "You're Elsa's secret admirer!" he exclaimed.

33

"Elsa's secret admirer?" the baker echoed, baffled.

"Of course!" Anna answered. "Why else would you be making her favorite cake?"

The baker stopped frowning as he realized the misunderstanding. Without saying a word, he pushed the heavy mixing bowl across the table to Anna. Unable to resist, she dipped her finger into the batter and tasted it. Her eyes widened in delight.

"Krumkake!" she said, thrilled. "My favorite!"

"Exactly," the baker replied.

Now it was Olaf's turn to look confused. "Wait, does that mean you're not Elsa's secret admirer?" he asked.

"I don't know anything about this secret admirer business," the baker said. "But Anna has been asking me to make krumkake for weeks."

"It's true," Anna nodded sheepishly. She'd forgotten all about it, but the sight of the baker lifting the first batch of delicious cakes from the hot pans was enough to remind her.

"I'm afraid we fell for a red herring," Anna replied. She pointed to the bowl of krumkake batter.

"Did someone say herring? I think Cook is making pickled herring for dinner," said the baker.

Anna scrunched her nose. She didn't

care for pickled herring, though Elsa liked it. Anna supposed it was only fair. If they were having Anna's favorite dessert, they could have Elsa's favorite dinner.

"So we keep looking?" Olaf asked enthusiastically.

"We keep looking," Anna said. Her stomach wasn't looking forward to dinner, but she was certainly looking forward to finding Elsa's secret admirer.

Chapter 4

Back on the hunt, Anna and Olaf crept through the castle passageways. They peeped into the portrait hall, the ballroom, and the library. There was nothing out of the ordinary in any of those rooms. Life in the castle seemed the same as always.

Just when Anna was beginning to

think they should look outside the castle, she heard a noise.

"Do you hear that, Olaf?" asked Anna. "It sounds like someone's singing."

Olaf tilted his head to listen. A soft voice drifted up into their hidden pass-age, humming a lovely tune. "Where's it coming from?" Olaf asked.

"Let's find out," said Anna.

She and Olaf sneaked along the corridor, following the sound. In a few moments, they reached the source.

"It's right next to us," Olaf whispered.

Anna searched for the nearest peephole. As soon as she found it, she looked into the room on the other side. It was the

castle sewing room. Maren, the royal dressmaker, was hard at work.

Maren hummed pleasantly to herself. Her kind blue eyes twinkled, and a strand of red hair slipped free from her bun. She stood in front of a beautiful ball gown on a dressmaker's dummy. The gown was pale lilac. Its beaded top shimmered in the light from the window. The full skirt fell from the waist to the floor in a flounce of silk. Maren grasped the bottom of the dress and began to pin up the hem.

"That's *some* gown," Anna murmured, impressed.

"Let me see!" Olaf said in a hushed voice.

Anna gave Olaf a boost so he could look through the opening.

"Oh," Olaf sighed, staring at the dress. "Pretty! Fit for a queen."

Anna thought for a moment, tapping her foot. "Olaf, you're a genius!" she said at last.

"Me?" asked Olaf with a goofy grin.

"Yes, you! You're exactly right. That dress *is* fit for a queen!" Anna replied happily. "It must be for Elsa! It's the perfect gift!" In her excitement, she leaned against the peephole wall. Unfortunately, the wall was also a hidden door! The door flew open and Anna stumbled into the sewing room. Olaf bounded after her

enthusiastically. He thought Anna had meant to catch Maren by surprise.

"Gotcha!" Olaf cried.

Startled, Maren threw her arms in the air, knocking over the dressmaker's dummy. The beautiful gown tipped over. Its puffy skirt covered Olaf in an unexpected wave of silk. He was practically wearing Elsa's dress!

"Oh, my!" Maren said, alarmed.

"I can't see!" Olaf yelled, bumbling under the heap of fabric. He waved his arms frantically. From where Anna stood, it looked like the dress was moving by itself.

Just then, Kai walked into the room.

"Is everyone okay?" he asked. "I heard all the noise and I— GHOST!" Kai shouted, pointing to the mysterious moving dress.

In the middle of the confusion, Anna giggled. "It's just Olaf." She lifted the dressmaker's dummy so Olaf could untangle himself from the dress.

"What is going on here?" Kai asked as Olaf climbed out from under the silky skirt.

"I was hoping someone would tell me," Maren said. "I was hemming Queen Elsa's new gown when suddenly these two burst through the wall." She pointed to Anna and Olaf.

"Have you two been sneaking around in the secret passages?" Kai scolded lightly.

Anna nodded ruefully. "Yes. Well, searching," she said.

"Yes, searching!" Olaf repeated.

"For Elsa's secret admirer," Anna explained.

"—and we found her!" Olaf exclaimed, pointing to Maren.

44

"Secret admirer?" Maren asked.

"You made Elsa this pretty dress!" Olaf said.

"It's my job to make beautiful dresses," Maren replied. "I'm the royal dressmaker."

Olaf and Anna exchanged a disappointed glance.

"So you didn't send her a love fish?" Olaf asked the dressmaker.

Maren frowned. She told Olaf that she had no idea what a love fish was, but she was fairly certain she hadn't sent one to the queen. "Besides, I like Elsa and that's not a secret. Doesn't everyone like the queen?" she asked.

"Of course!" said Olaf.

"It's true," Kai agreed. "But I guess

that makes it difficult to narrow down your list of possible admirers," he said to Anna and Olaf.

Anna knew Kai was right. If they were going to find out who was behind these gifts, they'd need more information. "I wish we had another clue," she said.

Maren propped her hands on her hips. "Well, if you two are done snooping, I'll get back to work," she said. The dressmaker returned to hemming Elsa's new gown.

Anna and Olaf headed back toward the open panel in the wall, but Kai stopped them with a look. "Why don't we all use the same door?" he said wryly, putting an

end to the day's sneaking. Kai closed the secret panel, then walked to the sewing room door and held it open for Anna and Olaf. Sheepishly, the princess and the snowman left the room.

"At least I got to try on the dress!" Olaf exclaimed.

47

Chapter 5

The next morning, Anna discovered that her wish for another clue had come true. As soon as the sun's rays spilled into her room, she scrambled out of bed. She didn't bother to brush her teeth, comb her hair, or even get dressed. Anna ran down the hallway, flew down the stairs, and raced out into the courtyard in her nightgown and slippers! She wasn't normally an early riser, but she wanted to know if the secret admirer had left another gift.

When Anna reached the courtyard, she looked at the gurgling water fountains. According to Kai, this was where the secret admirer had left the other presents for Elsa. Anna walked all the way around each of the fountains, hoping to find a clue. She was just about to give up her search when something unusual caught her eye. There, near the base of the last fountain, was a small purple crocus.

"That's odd," Anna murmured. The courtyard was paved in cobblestones. There was no place for crocuses to grow. Anna bent down to take a closer look. She noticed that the flower was stuck to a small cloth bag. "It's another gift for Elsa!" she exclaimed. She carefully picked up the bag and raced back inside the castle.

On her way to Elsa's bedroom, Anna ran into Olaf. He'd woken up early, too. Anna showed him the gift she'd found. Together they hurried to Elsa's room and knocked impatiently.

After a moment or two of knocking, Elsa came to the door. She blinked sleepily at Anna and Olaf. Elsa was surprised to see her sister that early. Anna usually liked to sleep late. "Is everything all right?" Elsa asked.

"Everything's perfect!" Anna replied. "There's another gift from You-Know-

Who." Eagerly, she handed the present to Elsa. "Go on, open it!"

Elsa studied the cloth sack carefully. She plucked the crocus from the outside and playfully tucked it behind her ear. Next, she untied the end of the bag. A tiny scrap of parchment slipped free. The handwriting on the parchment was familiar by now. It read:

A day with you would be like music to my ears!

Elsa opened the bag further. Inside was a beautiful wooden pan flute.

"Wow!" Anna said. "That's amazing!"

"It's really nice," Elsa responded, a little overwhelmed.

"What is it?" Olaf asked.

Elsa handed Olaf the bag. He gently took the flute out. It was made of eight slim wooden pipes tied together. Each of the pipes was a different length and made to play a different note. Olaf examined the instrument closely. He touched the smooth reddish wood with his fingers. He lifted the flute to his mouth excitedly and blew into the pipes. *TOOT! TOOT!*

Olaf squealed with delight. "The secret admirer must be someone who likes music."

"Actually, Olaf, that's not a bad guess," Anna said. "Like a troubadour or something."

"Exactly! Like a troubadour!" Olaf replied. "What's a troubadour?" he asked Anna.

"A troubadour is a traveling poet who sings songs and tells tales," she explained.

"Gee, what a great job!" Olaf said.

"If the secret admirer is a *traveling* poet, then no wonder we didn't find them in the castle!" Anna said.

"What do you mean, 'in the castle'?" Elsa asked.

"Well, Olaf and I, we might have . . . kind of . . . maybe accidentally . . . been . . . uh . . . investigating the identity of your secret admirer yesterday," Anna admitted.

"You investigated without me?" Elsa asked.

"We're sorry," Anna apologized. "We couldn't help ourselves."

"Plus, it was going to be a surprise!" Olaf added. "We were going to find the secret admirer and surprise you with LOVE!"

Elsa had to smile at Olaf's enthusiasm. "Well, I guess I can't object to that," she said. "But why don't you let me know the next time you go searching for a secret admirer—especially *my* secret admirer?"

"I think we can manage that," Anna replied lightheartedly.

"So, what did you discover yesterday?" Elsa asked.

Anna and Olaf were happy to share their investigation with Elsa. They described their adventures in the castle's secret passages.

Elsa listened to the facts and reviewed them thoroughly. She scratched her chin in thought. "Maybe you're right about traveling," she said. "Maybe we need to travel."

"You mean take the search outside the castle?" Anna asked.

"Yes," Elsa answered. "For example, the first gift was a fish—"

"—a love fish!" Olaf interrupted.

"Actually, a salmon," Anna said.

"Right," Elsa replied. "We know the salmon in Arendelle comes from Petra's Stream. So whoever caught it must have been there."

"Why didn't we think of that?" Olaf asked Anna.

It was Elsa who answered. "I guess some things just need a queen's touch," she responded playfully.

Chapter 6

A short while later, Elsa, Anna, and Olaf hiked through the forest just outside the village. The forest was full of tall, ancient trees. Their sturdy branches laced together overhead, forming a leafy green canopy. The morning sun filtered through the branches, painting the three friends in dappled light.

"I love the forest in springtime!" Olaf said. "Everything is just so green!"

Elsa liked it, too. It was always exciting to see the first plant push through the soil. Most of the fields around Arendelle were carpeted in crocuses, one of the first flowers to bloom each year.

Up ahead, Elsa, Anna, and Olaf saw a small clearing. As they approached, they could hear water splashing over rocks.

"Petra's Stream is just ahead," Anna said. Olaf eagerly hopped toward the clearing.

Elsa and Anna followed him. They walked through the line of trees into the open field. The grass sloped downward to the muddy banks of a babbling brook.

Silver-backed salmon streaked through the clear water.

"This is the place," Anna said.

Elsa knelt to examine the muddy ground. There were all sorts of tracks, from reindeer to rabbit, and too many footprints to count. A glance told Elsa that the stream was a busy place.

"Do you see the secret admirer's footprints?" Olaf asked.

"I'm not sure how we would recognize them, Olaf," Elsa replied. "We don't know what they look like."

"Maybe they're shaped like hearts," Olaf said. "After all, the secret admirer must be oozing with love!"

"Somehow I don't think so," Elsa chuckled. "But I do like your imagination."

"I've got something better than imagination," Anna said. She pointed to two people fishing in the stream a short distance away. "Maybe they saw our mystery person."

Elsa, Anna, and Olaf made their way to

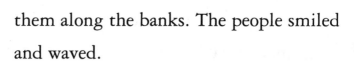

them along the banks. The people smiled and waved.

"Good afternoon, Queen Elsa, Princess Anna," said the woman. It was Elin, a fisherwoman Anna knew. "This is my friend Stefan."

Stefan inclined his head politely. "I'd greet the little fellow, too, but I don't know his name," he said.

"I'm Olaf!" Olaf interjected.

"Well, how can we help you, Olaf?" Elin asked.

"We're looking for a trooby . . . a trouba . . . a troopa . . . a poet," Olaf said, forgetting the word.

"A tuba?" Stefan asked.

"A troubadour," Anna said.

"Oh! Well, why didn't you say so?" Stefan responded. "Nope, we haven't seen a troubadour."

"Or a tuba," Elin added.

Anna told Elin and Stefan all about the mysterious gifts Elsa had received. She asked if they had seen anyone else fishing for salmon over the past day or so.

"We fish here every day, so we've seen plenty of folks fishing," Elin said. "But none like the little snow fellow described."

"Anyone new? Maybe someone who hasn't been here before?" Elsa asked.

"Now that you mention it, there was a new face a couple of days ago," Elin answered. "A young boy with dark hair."

"No tuba," Stefan pointed out. "But he

did have a dreamy look on his face."

"Maybe he's your poet," Elin suggested.

"Maybe," Anna said.

Elsa thanked Elin and Stefan for their help, while Olaf gave each of them a warm hug. Soon they were walking back through the forest with Anna leading the way. She was thinking about the investigation.

"Maybe one of the other gifts will give us more clues," Anna said. She thought about the second gift, the ice sculpture. Olaf had thought it meant that the secret admirer worked with snow. That wasn't such a bad idea. Maybe a visit to the ice harvesters would help shed some light on the mystery.

"Let's go to the frozen lake," Anna told

Elsa and Olaf. "I have a feeling the ice harvesters might know who carved that sculpture."

Anna, Olaf, and Elsa turned onto the trail that led to the mountains. Every step they took brought them closer to the tuba-playing, song-singing, fish-loving, ice-carving poet who was Elsa's biggest fan.

Chapter 7

Even though it was spring in Arendelle, it was still cold in the mountains. Snow dotted the rocky peaks and dusted the ground. The lake was frozen, and the ice harvesters were hard at work sawing through the ice, cutting it into blocks and loading it onto sleighs.

As Anna, Elsa, and Olaf stepped onto the icy surface of the lake, Anna rubbed her arms to keep warm. They hadn't planned to go to the lake, so she hadn't brought her cloak. The frosty air made her shiver, but she was the only one. Elsa didn't mind the cold, and Olaf—well, he was a snowman. He was in his element!

Kristoff was working alongside the other harvesters when he noticed Anna shivering. He walked over to her and offered her his coat.

"Won't you be cold?" Anna asked him.

"Me? Cold? Of course not! I've got ice practically running through my veins," Kristoff joked. "Besides, I've worked up a sweat with all this heavy lifting."

Anna gratefully accepted the coat and shrugged it on.

"What brings you to the mountains without a jacket?" Kristoff asked.

"Official detective business," Anna replied.

"Oh, brother," Kristoff said lightly. "Not that again. Once you get your teeth into a mystery, there's no letting it go."

"Precisely. So help me out or step aside," Anna said playfully.

"Who's the suspect?" Kristoff asked.

"Who says there's a suspect?" Anna said.

"There's *always* a suspect," Kristoff replied knowingly.

"It just so happens we're looking for

Elsa's secret admirer," Anna told him.

Kristoff looked at Elsa, his brow furrowed in thought. "That's a tough one," he said. "Everyone loves the queen."

"Well, this person has a few unique characteristics," Elsa explained.

"Like what?" asked Kristoff.

"We think the secret admirer is a tuba-playing trouba!" Olaf blurted out.

"—dour. Troubadour," Anna said, finishing the word. "And he doesn't play the tuba."

Kristoff looked puzzled. He had no idea what Olaf and Anna were talking about.

Elsa noticed Kristoff's confusion. She told him about her three gifts and their recent visit to Petra's Stream.

"Oh," Kristoff said when she was done. "That makes sense. Sort of."

"I guess we're looking for someone who likes to carve ice sculptures," Elsa explained.

"That could be anyone around here," Kristoff said. "Especially with the big contest coming up."

"Yes, the contest!" Anna said. "The Spring Sculpture Classic!"

Every spring, Arendelle held an ice-sculpting competition at the frozen lake. Anna and Elsa loved to watch the villagers with their chisels and picks. In just an hour or so, contestants transformed regular blocks of ice into fantastic creations!

"Some of the harvesters have been

practicing all week," Kristoff said. "I can show you some of their work?"

"Lead the way," Anna replied.

Kristoff showed Anna, Elsa, and Olaf to the western edge of the lake. There, away from the well-choreographed assembly line of ice harvesters, was a circle of ice carvings. The statues were all different sizes, and most of them were unfinished.

"It's just for practice," Kristoff explained. "A lot of the harvesters have been trying out new tools."

Elsa walked between the unfinished sculptures. Even though they were just for practice, some of them were very good. "It's amazing what people can do with ice!" she said.

73

"You don't say," Anna replied, winking at her sister. She knew that Elsa could do some pretty amazing things with ice, too.

Elsa touched several of the more complicated carvings. Then she walked over to a sculpture that looked slightly familiar. It was a practice carving of a lady's head.

"Anna, come look at this one," Elsa said.

Olaf bounced over to Elsa. "Hey, that looks like the secret admirer's gift!"

Anna studied the sculpture. "These are the same chisel marks!" she said.

"That means the secret admirer must have been here," Elsa reasoned.

"Kristoff, do you know who carved this?" asked Anna.

"I don't," Kristoff said. "But the sculpture's pretty rough. It was probably made by someone who has just started carving."

"Maybe someone young?" Anna asked. "An apprentice?"

Kristoff thought for a moment. "Well, there's Fredmund. He started his apprenticeship a week or so ago," he explained.

"Does he have dark hair?" Elsa asked.

"Yeah. How did you know?" asked Kristoff.

Elsa and Anna exchanged a look. The description of the boy matched what Elin and Stefan had told them. "I think this Fredmund might be our man," Anna said.

"Boy," Kristoff told her. "He's only seven."

Elsa thought back to the wobbly handwriting and the simple notes left by the secret admirer. There was something

very sweet about the gifts, and also something youthful. If her secret admirer turned out to be seven years old, everything made sense.

"Do you know where Fredmund lives?" she asked.

"I'm not sure," Kristoff answered. "But I think someone said he lives near the outer lake."

"The outer lake?" Elsa said. "That's a pretty big place."

Anna thought there had to be a way to narrow down the search for Fredmund. "Hold on a second," she told Elsa. "Did you bring the secret admirer's third gift?"

Elsa nodded. She reached into the

pocket of her dress and pulled out the pan flute. Anna took the flute from her sister and inspected it closely. She turned the instrument over in her hands, touching the smooth red wood. Anna had seen that color of wood before. It was very familiar.

"Look at this," she said, holding the pan flute out to Elsa.

"That's made from red alder wood," Kristoff said.

"You're right," Elsa said. "And there's a red alder grove on the northern shore of the outer lake!"

"Then we know exactly where to look next," Anna said.

Kristoff looked from one sister to the

other, impressed. "You two make a great team."

"Don't forget me!" Olaf said. "I'm on the team, too!"

"Olaf, you're unforgettable," Kristoff said with a smile.

Chapter 8

Elsa, Anna, and Olaf left Kristoff to continue his work in the mountains. As they descended the rocky mountain trails, the air grew warmer again. Anna was relieved. She'd given Kristoff back his coat and was happy to enjoy the spring afternoon. The snowcapped mountain peaks disappeared behind fluffy white clouds. Anna noticed that the ground beneath her feet was soft and green again.

The walk to the outer lake took a little more than an hour, but the friends didn't mind. There was so much to see along the way. They strolled along the length of a narrow fjord, watching the seawater flow between the steep cliffs.

On the way to the red alder grove, Anna thought about Elsa's secret admirer. She was curious about the person who had chosen such unique gifts for her sister. It was clear that he enjoyed ice carving, but what did the other gifts mean? Did he really like to fish? Did he play the pan flute? She and Olaf had guessed so many things about him. She wondered if they would turn out to be true. Could you really know a person by the gifts he gave?

At last they reached the red alder grove. The tall, thin trees were clustered together on the northern banks of the outer lake. Their trunks were slim and knotty with pale gray bark. The wood inside was the light reddish color that made the pan flute unique. Shiny green leaves unfurled from the branches overhead.

The grove was quiet except for the rustling of the wind through the leaves. Anna, Elsa, and Olaf could hear the faint sound of the lake lapping against the shore. The three friends threaded their way through the trees and onto the bank. By the lake was a small cottage with blue

shutters, and a colorful garden of spring flowers in front. Through the windows Anna, Elsa, and Olaf could see people moving around inside.

Suddenly, the door to the cottage flew open. A young, dark-haired boy raced outside. He wore a bedsheet tied like a cape around his shoulders. In his left hand he held a wooden sword. The boy didn't notice the three visitors on the shore. He ran to the edge of the lake, swinging his sword left and right. He was engaged in a duel with an imaginary monster.

"Take that . . . and that! Don't worry, my queen, we'll save the village together!" the boy said, lost in his play.

Anna and Elsa smiled at the fun the boy was having. It reminded them of the games they used to play when they were little. Elsa tapped Anna and Olaf on the shoulder. She motioned for them to hide behind a tree with her. Elsa didn't want to interrupt the boy when he was using his

imagination. This had to be Fredmund! Who else would be creative enough to give her a frozen fish?

"What do you say we give him a surprise?" Elsa said to Anna.

"What did you have in mind?" Anna asked.

Elsa twirled her fingers through the air. A cluster of snowflakes and ice crystals began to form. Elsa guided the crystals out to the banks of the lake. There, she shaped them into the form of a huge ice dragon. If the boy wanted to fight a monster, she'd give him one! But Fredmund didn't notice. He was busy jousting with shadows.

Moments later, the ice dragon was

finished. It was nearly ten feet tall, and its wings were spread as if it were about to fly. The afternoon sun glittered across the statue's back. It was very impressive.

"Ahem," Elsa said, clearing her throat.

Fredmund whirled around at the sound. When he saw the statue, his eyes grew wide with fright! He was absolutely shocked. "AHHHHHHHHHHHHH!" he cried.

"Uh-oh," Elsa said ruefully. "I guess my surprise was a little too much."

Fredmund dropped his sword and took off running. "Save me!" he yelled, flailing his arms.

Elsa dashed out from behind the tree.

"Wait!" she called, running toward him.

Fredmund glanced up to see Queen Elsa hurrying over to him. He was thunderstruck. Between the queen and the dragon, he was having an afternoon he'd never forget! He was so startled, he tripped and lost his balance. Elsa reached Fredmund just in time. She grabbed his cape and kept him from falling.

"Your Majesty!" Fredmund gasped.

"I'm sorry I scared you. It's just an ice sculpture. I made it for you," Elsa explained. "I saw you were pretending, so I thought I'd give you a pretend monster."

Fredmund's ears began to turn bright red. "Wow, it looks so real," he said,

calming down. But he was embarrassed. He'd been pretending to rescue the village from a scary monster. Instead, *he* was the one who'd gotten scared. "I guess *you* rescued *me.*"

Elsa smiled. "Everyone needs a rescue sometimes," she said. "Queens and princesses get to do the rescuing, too. Take my sister, Anna, for example. She saved me once."

Fredmund's eyes brightened. "Is Princess Anna here, too?"

At the sound of her name, Anna popped out from behind the tree with Olaf. "You bet I am," she said. "And this is our friend Olaf."

Olaf bounded over to shake hands with Fredmund. "It's a snowman!" the boy said excitedly.

"Of course!" Olaf replied happily. "Do you like warm hugs? I give all my friends warm hugs."

Elsa and Anna nodded encouragingly at Fredmund. Fredmund opened his arms wide, and Olaf snuggled into them. The boy giggled. Hugging Olaf was actually pretty cold, but it was worth it.

When Olaf was finished hugging him, Fredmund said, "I can't believe I just hugged a snowman!" He clapped his hands together. "I can't believe I just met Queen Elsa and Princess Anna!" He

dusted himself off and straightened his cape. "Oh! I almost forgot! We haven't really been introduced!"

The boy swept into a deep bow. "My name is Fredmund, but you can call me Freddy," he said proudly.

Elsa curtsied in return. "It's lovely to meet you, Freddy," she said. "And I have a question for you."

"What's that?" Freddy said.

"Do you know who might be leaving me gifts?" Elsa asked.

Freddy blushed and looked down at his toes. In front of Elsa, he felt very shy.

"It's okay, you can tell me," Elsa said gently.

Freddy nodded. He gathered all his courage and looked up at Elsa. "My mother always says to tell the truth," he said hesitantly. "I'm your secret admirer."

Chapter 9

"AHA!" Olaf shouted, overjoyed. They'd been looking for Elsa's secret admirer for days, and they'd finally found him!

Elsa smiled warmly at Fredmund. "It was very nice of you to send me those gifts," she said. "What made you decide to do that?"

"Well, you're just the neatest lady around!" Freddy gushed. "Oh! I almost forgot!" He pulled a shiny pebble from his pocket. Freddy offered the pebble to Elsa and got down on one knee. "Queen Elsa, will you marry me?" he asked politely.

"Freddy, that's very sweet, but why do you want to marry me?" Elsa asked.

"I don't know. I heard it's what you do when you like someone," Freddy answered, shrugging. "But really I guess it's because you can do such cool stuff with ice." He gazed wistfully at the huge, beautiful dragon statue just a few feet away and sighed. "I'm in the ice-carving contest tomorrow, and I'm a little nervous. I guess I was hoping you could teach me?"

"Of course I can teach you," Elsa said. "We don't have to be married for that."

"We don't?" Fredmund asked innocently.

Elsa shook her head. "All we have to do is be friends," she explained.

Freddy perked up. "We're already friends, aren't we?"

"Absolutely!" Elsa responded.

Freddy told Elsa, Anna, and Olaf all about his hopes for the competition. He'd been practicing to create a sculpture of Elsa, but making people out of ice was very hard. He felt his work wasn't very good compared to some of the other ice harvesters' sculptures.

Anna offered Freddy a bit of friendly

advice. "When something is really hard at first, I practice it a lot," she said. "After a while, it gets easier."

"I know!" Freddy replied, nodding enthusiastically. "That's what my mom said, but I've been practicing and practicing, and I haven't gotten any better."

"How long have you practiced?" Anna asked.

"Days!" Freddy sighed. His shoulders slumped in disappointment. "I'm still not good enough," he told them sadly.

"Cheer up!" Olaf said.

"It's true," said Elsa gently. "Some things take time. But you shouldn't think

that you're not good enough. Of course you are!"

"You really think so?" Freddy asked.

"I know so," Elsa replied. "In fact, I have an idea."

"What's that?" asked Freddy eagerly.

"People are hard to carve. Why not start with a simpler idea?" Elsa suggested.

Freddy liked that, but he wasn't sure what else to make. "There's so much to choose from!" he exclaimed. "I could make absolutely anything! What should I do?"

Olaf struck a pose and cleared his throat.

"Hmm," Anna said. "A snowman would be easy to make. His body is shaped

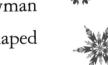

like two circles, and he has an oval for a head."

"Hey, you're right!" Freddy said. He looked carefully at Olaf and blinked. "I can do that!"

"Fredmund!" a voice interrupted. "Time for dinner!"

Elsa looked up to see a woman standing in the door of the little cottage by the lake. She held a hand over her kind brown eyes to shield them from the setting sun. She quickly scanned the banks of the river, looking for her son.

"Mom! Over here!" Freddy called.

Freddy's mother smiled and walked toward him. She stopped suddenly, however, when she spotted the queen, the princess, a snowman, and an enormous ice dragon! "Oh my goodness!" she exclaimed.

"Don't worry, Mom! The dragon's not real!" Freddy told her.

"But we are!" Olaf said brightly.

"I can see that," Freddy's mother said

softly. She dropped into a curtsy before Elsa and Anna. "Pleased to meet you, Your Majesty, Your Highness. I'm Maarika. I hope Fredmund hasn't been bothering you."

"I remembered all my manners, Mom! I promise!" Freddy said.

"He's been very polite," Elsa assured her. "And in return I'd like to help him at the ice-carving contest tomorrow. If that's okay with you."

"Please, Mom?" Freddy asked.

"That's very generous of you, Queen Elsa. We'd love that," said Maarika. "What do you say, Fredmund?"

"Thank you, Queen Elsa!" Freddy answered, thrilled.

Maarika stepped forward and ruffled her son's hair. "Okay, mister. Go inside and wash up for dinner. Your dad is waiting for you," she told him.

Freddy gave Elsa, Anna, and Olaf a gallant bow before racing toward the cottage.

Chapter 10

The next morning at the frozen lake, Anna had remembered to bring her cloak. She was toasty warm standing on the ice next to Elsa, Kristoff, Freddy, and Olaf. Freddy's parents watched from the icy banks with the other spectators. Everyone from the village had come to see the Spring Sculpture Classic.

This year, ten contestants were participating. Each was given a three-foot-tall block of ice and two hours to create a masterpiece.

Freddy stood anxiously in front of his ice block. Even though Elsa, Anna, and Olaf were there to encourage him, he would have to do all of the carving on his own.

"I'm really nervous, Queen Elsa," Freddy said. His hands were sweaty and his throat felt dry.

"It's okay, Freddy," Elsa said. "Just remember your plan. You only have to make two circles and an oval."

Just then, the whistle blew and the

competition began. Freddy picked up his mallet and chisel in his sweaty palms. Olaf posed dramatically next to the block of ice. All Freddy had to do was copy his pose.

"Go, Freddy! You can do it!" Anna said.

Freddy began to chip away at the block of ice. Ice carving was slow and steady work.

Bit by bit, the block began to take shape. First, Freddy knew that he had to make the block round. He used his chisel to smooth out the angular corners.

"Good thinking, Freddy!" Elsa told him.

Freddy smiled briefly and turned back

to his work. For the next hour, his brow was furrowed in concentration. All that could be heard was the tapping of his mallet against his chisel. *Tap, tap, tap.*

Soon Elsa could see that Freddy's block had three separate sections. The bottom had been carved into two circles, and the top was beginning to look like an oval.

Freddy stepped back from the block to take a look at his work. He set down his tools and wiped his palms on his coat. After a moment, his face fell.

"What's wrong, Freddy?" Elsa asked.

"It's just not as good as the others," he answered, looking around at the statues of

the other contestants. To him, they looked far more complicated than his.

"Sure it is," Elsa said.

Freddy shook his head. "My circles are lopsided," he said disappointedly. "And you can barely tell that's an oval."

"You're still learning, Freddy," Elsa reminded him. "You're doing a really great job."

"I wish I had your powers," Freddy said to Elsa sadly. "Everything you make is beautiful."

Elsa knelt so she could look Freddy in the eye. "Freddy, I had to learn how to use my powers, too," she explained. "I spent a long time learning how to control them,

and sometimes things still don't always turn out as planned."

"Really?" Freddy asked, amazed.

Elsa nodded. Then she whispered, "I'll tell you another secret, too. I'm not the only one with powers."

"You're not?" Freddy said. His eyes widened with wonder.

"No. You have powers, too," she told him.

"I do?" asked Freddy, astonished.

"Yes, but your powers are different from mine. You have the power of creativity and imagination," Elsa explained.

"You're just saying that to make me feel better," Freddy said.

"No, I mean it," Elsa replied gently. "You gave me some very creative gifts. Most people think queens just like flowers and jewelry, but you gave me things that were unique. Things you made with your own hands."

"I did, didn't I?" Freddy said, remembering.

"Did you carve that flute all by yourself?" asked Elsa.

"I did. My dad showed me how to make it last year," he answered.

"And you carved it from a block of wood, right?" Elsa said.

"Yes," Freddy replied.

"Maybe you can use some of your

wood-carving skills to carve this block of ice," Elsa suggested.

Freddy studied the block of ice for a moment. He walked all the way around it, running his fingers over the frosty surface. Finally, he reached into his pocket and pulled out a wood whittling tool. He slid it carefully across the frozen block. The tool shaved off a thin layer of ice.

"It worked!" Freddy exclaimed.

Elsa smiled warmly in response.

Freddy went to work with the whittling tool. Within minutes, a pile of ice shavings had built up at his feet.

"Thatta boy, Freddy!" Anna said, cheering him on.

"Wow!" Olaf said as the ice block was transformed. "It looks just like me!"

Now that Freddy was working steadily, the minutes slipped by. Before anyone knew it, the final whistle blew. The contest was over! The ice carvers set down their tools and stood proudly beside their creations. Freddy beamed. His Olaf sculpture was almost a perfect likeness, right down to the pointy carrot nose!

Two judges walked across the lake to inspect each of the sculptures. When it was time for them to look at Freddy's work, he bowed politely. The judges circled the statue and smiled.

"Was that a good sign, Queen Elsa?" Freddy asked quietly.

"I hope so," Elsa answered.

"Finger crossed," Anna added.

"Toes, too!" said Olaf. "Oh, wait, I don't have toes."

Everyone waited patiently while the judges completed their inspections. They discussed each of the sculptures privately. Soon they were ready to announce the results.

"And the first-place winner of this year's Spring Sculpture Classic is . . . Thorken Eriksson!" said the head judge. Thorken was one of the ice harvesters. He'd been entering the contest for years. This was his first win. The spectators cheered.

As Thorken approached the judges to collect his trophy, the other winners were

announced. Freddy didn't place, but he got an honorable mention. He whooped when his name was called, and hurried to collect his ribbon.

Once he received his award, Freddy ran over to hug his parents. Then he barreled back to Elsa, Anna, and Olaf. He threw his arms around Elsa in a giant bear hug that nearly knocked her over.

Elsa smiled and hugged him tight. "I'm so proud of you, Freddy!" she said.

"Me too! I mean . . . thank you!" he said, remembering his manners. "I didn't win, but who else can say he got ice-carving lessons from the queen? I'll remember this day forever!"

Elsa, Anna, and Olaf laughed.

115

"I'll remember it, too," Elsa said fondly. "It's the day my secret admirer became my friend."

*

Later that day, after Freddy had returned to the outer lake with his parents, Elsa, Anna, and Olaf were walking back to the castle. As they crossed a field of spring crocuses, Elsa noticed that Anna looked slightly let down.

"What's wrong, Anna?" she asked.

"Nothing," Anna replied.

Elsa arched an eyebrow. She didn't believe that for a second. She fixed Anna with a look.

"Well, I guess I miss it," Anna said.

"Miss what?" asked Elsa.

"The mystery of your secret admirer," Anna answered.

"You and Olaf will have to find something else to search for," Elsa said.

"I guess so," Anna responded. The sisters walked in silence for a moment.

"Elsa?"

"Yes."

"With all this secret admirer talk, do you ever wish you had someone special?" Anna asked.

Elsa threw an arm around Anna's shoulder. "But I do have someone special," she said. "My sister!"

Anna smiled.

"And me!" Olaf chimed in.

"And you, Olaf," Elsa agreed. "One can never have too many special friends."